AF305032

MACMILLAN COLLECTOR'S LIBRARY

# Weekly Planner

MACMILLAN COLLECTOR'S LIBRARY

# MONTH

1

2

3

4

5

6

7

8

9

10

11

12

13

14

15

16

17

18

19

20

21

22

23

24

25

26

27

28

29

30

31

1
2
3
4
5
6
7
8
9
10
11
12
13
14
15
16
17
18
19
20
21
22
23
24
25
26
27
28
29
30
31

# MONTH

1
2
3
4
5
6
7
8
9
10
11
12
13
14
15
16
17
18
19
20
21
22
23
24
25
26
27
28
29
30
31

1
2
3
4
5
6
7
8
9
10
11
12
13
14
15
16
17
18
19
20
21
22
23
24
25
26
27
28
29
30
31

1
2
3
4
5
6
7
8
9
10
11
12
13
14
15
16
17
18
19
20
21
22
23
24
25
26
27
28
29
30
31

1
2
3
4
5
6
7
8
9
10
11
12
13
14
15
16
17
18
19
20
21
22
23
24
25
26
27
28
29
30
31

# MONTH

1
2
3
4
5
6
7
8
9
10
11
12
13
14
15
16
17
18
19
20
21
22
23
24
25
26
27
28
29
30
31

1
2
3
4
5
6
7
8
9
10
11
12
13
14
15
16
17
18
19
20
21
22
23
24
25
26
27
28
29
30
31

1

2

3

4

5

6

7

8

9

10

11

12

13

14

15

16

17

18

19

20

21

22

23

24

25

26

27

28

29

30

31

1
2
3
4
5
6
7
8
9
10
11
12
13
14
15
16
17
18
19
20
21
22
23
24
25
26
27
28
29
30
31

---

1
2
3
4
5
6
7
8
9
10
11
12
13
14
15
16
17
18
19
20
21
22
23
24
25
26
27
28
29
30
31

*Being thus decked out, she got up into her coach; but her godmother, above all things, commanded her not to stay till after midnight, telling her, at the same time, that if she stayed at the ball one moment longer, her coach would be a pumpkin again, her horses mice, her coachman a rat, her footmen lizards, and her clothes become just as they were before.*

‘CINDERELLA’, *Grimms’ Fairy Tales*

MONTH

You must be the best judge of your
own happiness.

JANE AUSTEN, *Emma*

MONTH

> *Hurry long strides*
> *and you never travel far.*
>
> LAO TZU, *Tao Te Ching*

# MONTH

We can't behave like people in novels,
though, can we?

EDITH WHARTON, *The Age of Innocence*

MONTH

*This above all: to thine own self be true.*

WILLIAM SHAKESPEARE, *Hamlet*

*This smoke rose up to the clouds and, stretching over the sea and the shore, formed a thick mist, which caused the fisherman much astonishment. When all the smoke was out of the jar it gathered itself together and became a thick mass in which appeared a genie, twice as large as the largest giant. When he saw such a terrible-looking monster, the fisherman would have run away, but he trembled so with fright he could not move a step.*

MONTH

'Bah!' said Scrooge, 'Humbug!'
CHARLES DICKENS, *A Christmas Carol*

MONTH

In little is contentment.

LAO TZU, *Tao Te Ching*

MONTH

*As I must do something or go mad,*
*I write this diary.*

BRAM STOKER, *Dracula*

MONTH

*Shall we go on dancing?*

RYUNOSUKE AKUTAGAWA, 'THE BALL'

*A large hedge of thorns soon grew round
the palace, and every year it became higher
and thicker; till at last the old palace was
surrounded and hidden, so that not even
the roof or the chimneys could be seen.
But there went a report through all the
land of the beautiful sleeping Briar Rose
(for so the king's daughter was called),
so that, from time to time, several kings'
sons came, and tried to break through
the thicket into the palace.*

'THE SLEEPING BEAUTY',
*Grimms' Fairy Tales*

# MONTH

*What madness is it this time?*

MIGUEL DE CERVANTES, *Don Quixote*

MONTH

Live! Live the wonderful life
that is in you!

OSCAR WILDE, *The Picture of Dorian Gray*

MONTH

Next to trying and winning, the best thing is trying and failing.

MONTH

*Tomorrow to fresh woods, and pastures new.*

JOHN MILTON, 'LYCIDAS'

*As soon as the shadow of the night had fallen, we set forth again, at first with the same caution, but presently with more boldness, standing our full height and stepping out at a good pace of walking. The way was very intricate, lying up the steep sides of mountains and along the brows of cliffs; clouds had come in with the sunset, and the night was dark and cool; so that I walked without much fatigue, but in continual fear of falling and rolling down the mountains, and with no guess at our direction.*

ROBERT LOUIS STEVENSON, *Kidnapped*

MONTH

> *But the stranger stood there,*
> *perfectly silent and still.*

H. G. WELLS, *The Invisible Man*

# MONTH

Let your soul stand cool and composed before
a million universes.

WALT WHITMAN, *Leaves of Grass*

A thing of beauty is a joy for ever.

JOHN KEATS, 'ENDYMION'

MONTH

> *If music be the food of love, play on.*
> WILLIAM SHAKESPEARE, *Twelfth Night*

*Happily for her companion, she wanted
no answer. Her mind was entirely
self-engrossed. She was in a reverie
of sweet remembrances.*

JANE AUSTEN, *Mansfield Park*

*I thank whatever gods may be*
*For my unconquerable soul.*

W. E. HENLEY, 'INVICTUS'

# MONTH

'Come here,' she said in a chill, hoarse voice.

MARJORIE BOWEN, 'TWILIGHT'

*Do we not need the tea-room more
than ever?*

OKAKURA KAKUZO, *The Book of Tea*

*I don't care about truth. I want
some happiness.*

F. SCOTT FITZGERALD,
*The Beautiful and Damned*

*Then the glass one day answered the queen,*
*when she went to look in it as usual:*
*'Thou, queen, art fair, and beauteous to see,*
*But Snow White is lovelier far than thee!'*

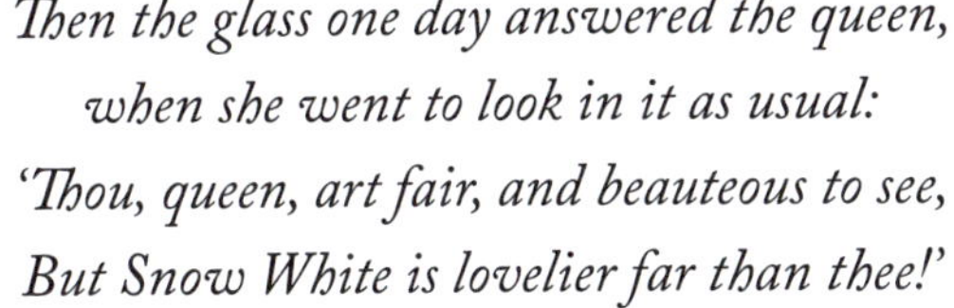

'SNOW WHITE', *Grimms' Fairy Tales*

We are such stuff as dreams are made on.

WILLIAM SHAKESPEARE, *The Tempest*

MONTH

> Beside the nettle, ever grows the cure
> for its sting.

MARY SEACOLE, *The Wonderful Adventures of Mrs Seacole in Many Lands*

MONTH

Double, double toil and trouble;
Fire burn and cauldron bubble.

WILLIAM SHAKESPEARE, *Macbeth*

MONTH

The Master said: 'Be loyal and stand by your words.'

CONFUCIUS, *The Analects*

*If gardeners had been developing from
the beginning of the world by natural
selection they would have evolved most
probably into some kind of invertebrate.
After all, for what purpose has a
gardener a back? Apparently only so that
he can straighten it at times, and say:
'My back does ache!'*

KAREL ČAPEK, *The Gardener's Year*

MONTH

*Mary wished to say something very sensible,
but knew not how.*

JANE AUSTEN, *Pride and Prejudice*

MONTH

*Mr. Holmes, they were the footprints of
a gigantic hound!*

ARTHUR CONAN DOYLE,
*The Hound of the Baskervilles*

MONTH

*True courage is in facing danger when
you are afraid.*

L. FRANK BAUM, *The Wizard of Oz*

Once upon a time there were three bears . . .

F. A. STEEL, *English Fairy Tales*

*One of the big trees had been partly chopped through, and standing beside it, with an uplifted axe in his hands, was a man made entirely of tin. His head and arms and legs were jointed upon his body, but he stood perfectly motionless, as if he could not stir at all. Dorothy looked at him in amazement, and so did the Scarecrow, while Toto barked sharply and made a snap at the tin legs, which hurt his teeth.*

L. FRANK BAUM, *The Wizard of Oz*

*I dare say . . . My heart knows who
it is I love.*

ANTON CHEKHOV, 'THE HORSE-STEALERS'

# MONTH

It is not down in any map; true places
never are.

HERMAN MELVILLE, *Moby-Dick*

MONTH

*We have a great deal more kindness
than is ever spoken.*

RALPH WALDO EMERSON, 'FRIENDSHIP'

MONTH

*Idols must not be touched; the gilt sticks
to the fingers.*

GUSTAVE FLAUBERT, *Madame Bovary*

*The church is calm enough, I am sure; but it might be a steam-power loom in full action, for any sedative effect it has on me. I am too far gone for that. The rest is all a more or less incoherent dream.*

CHARLES DICKENS, *David Copperfield*

MONTH

Yet through all these changes she had
remained, she reflected, fundamentally
the same.

VIRGINIA WOOLF, *Orlando*

*It was the sweetest, most mysterious-looking place anyone could ever imagine.*

FRANCES HODGSON BURNETT,
*The Secret Garden*

MONTH

> 'Can't repeat the past?' he cried incredulously.
> 'Why of course you can!'

F. SCOTT FITZGERALD, *The Great Gatsby*

*No hero is immune from the whims of the gods, it seems.*

CARL WITT, 'BELLEROPHON'

*Oh! it was grand. And it would all
have gone on being grand if he had not
unfortunately, while looking round to enjoy
the scenery, taken just one step more than
there was any necessity for, and walked off
the punt altogether. The pole was firmly
fixed in the mud, and he was left clinging
to it while the punt drifted away.*

JEROME K. JEROME, *Three Men in a Boat*

MONTH

She belonged in this land of rising towers.
She was an American.

NELLA LARSEN, *Passing*

*If you aren't free of yourself
how will you ever become yourself?*

LAO TZU, *Tao Te Ching*

MONTH

*All animals are equal, but some animals are more equal than others.*

GEORGE ORWELL, *Animal Farm*

MONTH

> *Beware; for I am fearless, and therefore powerful.*

MARY SHELLEY, *Frankenstein*

*The Caterpillar and Alice looked at each
other for some time in silence: at last the
Caterpillar took the hookah out of its mouth,
and addressed her in a languid, sleepy voice.*

*'Who are* you?' *said the Caterpillar.
This was not an encouraging opening for
a conversation. Alice replied, rather shyly,
'I – I hardly know, sir, just at present – at
least I know who I* was *when I got up this
morning, but I think I must have been
changed several times since then.'*

*'What do you mean by that?' said the
Caterpillar sternly. 'Explain yourself!'*

*'I can't explain* myself, *I'm afraid, sir,'
said Alice, 'because I'm not myself, you see.'*

MONTH

We sighed and fainted on the sofa.

JANE AUSTEN, 'LOVE AND FRIENDSHIP'

MONTH

It is a curious fact, but nobody ever
is seasick – on land.

JEROME K. JEROME, *Three Men in a Boat*

MONTH

*He rushed with outstretched hands to seize her, but clutched only air.*

CHARLOTTE RIDDELL, 'THE OLD HOUSE IN VAUXHALL WALK'

MONTH

Bobby knew, as well as any man, that it was the dinner-hour.

ELEANOR ATKINSON, *Greyfriars Bobby*

Arthur Watts . 30

*Ladies retire to the drawing-room and gather round quite inadequate fire. Coffee. I perform my usual sleight-of-hand, transferring large piece of candy-sugar from saucer to handbag, for Vicky's benefit. (Query: Why do people living in same neighbourhood as myself obtain without difficulty minor luxuries that I am totally unable to procure? Reply to this, if pursued to logical conclusion, appears to point to inadequate housekeeping on my part.)*

E. M. DELAFIELD,
*Diary of a Provincial Lady*

_It is said that strife in an army will sap its victory._

SUN TZU, *The Art of War*

'How delightful to see you!' said Clarissa.
She said it to every one.

VIRGINIA WOOLF, *Mrs Dalloway*

MONTH

Frayed I may be, but frayed rather from
my armour than from age.

MIGUEL DE CERVANTES, *Don Quixote*

MONTH

He kindly pressed my hand, and
went. Now I was happy again . . .

ANNE BRONTË, *Agnes Grey*

‘It is certain,’ exclaimed my uncle in a
tone of triumph. ‘But silence, do you hear
me? silence upon the whole subject; and
let no one get before us in this design of
discovering the centre of the earth.’

JULES VERNE, *Journey to the
Centre of the Earth*

MONTH

*Character is not cut in marble – it is not something solid and unalterable.*

GEORGE ELIOT, *Middlemarch*

MONTH

*Your name is Jean Valjean. Now shall I tell you who you are?*

VICTOR HUGO, *Les Misérables*

MONTH

*I will tell my story, and my reader shall judge for me.*

MARY SHELLEY, 'THE MORTAL IMMORTAL'

*Tomorrow! magic word of promise rare,*
*What witchery inheres in thy sweet name.*

CARRIE WILLIAMS CLIFFORD, 'TOMORROW'

MONTH

*You love me, and speak of parting. Never!*

KATE CHOPIN, 'WISER THAN A GOD'

'What a noble bird I see above me!
Her beauty is without equal, the hue of
her plumage exquisite. If only her voice
is as sweet as her looks are fair, she ought
without doubt to be queen of the birds.'
The crow was hugely flattered by this,
and just to show the fox that she could
sing she gave a loud caw. Down came the
cheese, of course, and the fox, snatching it
up, said, 'You have a voice, madam, I see.
What you want is wits.'

# NOTES

# NOTES

# NOTES

# NOTES

# TO DO LIST

# TO DO LIST

# TO DO LIST

All the quotes featured in this planner are chosen from books published by Macmillan Collector's Library. We publish classic novels, short stories, plays, poetry, works of non-fiction and children's books.

The short stories and poems come from these curated anthologies and collections:

*Grimms' Fairy Tales*

*Arabian Nights*
edited by Andrew Lang

*Parties and Passions: Classic Short Stories from Around the World*
edited by Elena Richards

*Poems for Travellers*
edited by Gaby Morgan

*Leaves of Grass*
by Walt Whitman

*Selected Poems*
by John Keats

*Poems for Happiness*
edited by Gaby Morgan

*Classic Horror Stories*
edited by David Stuart Davies

*English Fairy Tales*
edited by F. A. Steel

*In the Ravine & Other Stories*
by Anton Chekhov

*Finding Happiness*
by Zachary Seager

*Greek Myths: Heroes and Heroines*
edited by Jean Menzies

*Sanditon, Lady Susan & The History of England*
by Jane Austen

*Irish Ghost Stories*
edited by David Stuart Davies

*Standing Her Ground: Classic Short Stories
by Trailblazing Women*
edited by Harriet Sanders

*Women of the Harlem Renaissance:
Poems and Stories*
edited by Marissa Constantinou

*Aesop's Fables*

Discover the full range at
panmacmillan.com/mcl

First published 2026 by Macmillan Collector's Library
an imprint of Pan Macmillan
The Smithson, 6 Briset Street, London ECIM 5NR
*EU representative:* Macmillan Publishers Ireland Ltd, 1st Floor,
The Liffey Trust Centre, 117–126 Sheriff Street Upper,
Dublin 1, DOI YC43
Associated companies throughout the world

ISBN 978-1-0350-7221-7



Endpaper pattern by Andrew Davidson
Front and back cover © Bridgeman Images
Printed and bound in China by Imago

Visit **www.panmacmillan.com** to read more
about all our books and to buy them.